KOOKABURRA

Retold by STEVEN ANDERSON

Illustrated by DAN TAYLOR

CANTATA
LEARNING
MANKATO, MINNESOTA

WWW.CANTATALEARNING.COM

CANTATA LEARNING

MANKATO, MINNESOTA

Published by Cantata Learning
1710 Roe Crest Drive
North Mankato, MN 56003
www.cantatalearning.com

Library of Congress Control Number: 2014957024
978-1-63290-278-8 (hardcover/CD)
978-1-63290-430-0 (paperback/CD)
978-1-63290-472-0 (paperback)

Kookaburra by Steven Anderson
Illustrated by Dan Taylor

Book design, Tim Palin Creative
Editorial direction, Flat Sole Studio
Executive musical production and direction, Elizabeth Draper
Music arranged and produced by Steven C Music

Printed in the United States of America.

VISIT

WWW.CANTATALEARNING.COM/ACCESS-OUR-MUSIC

TO SING ALONG TO THE SONG

What is a kookaburra? It's a bird that lives in the countries of **Australia** and **New Guinea**.

Its **call** sounds like a person laughing loudly.

Now turn the page, and sing along.

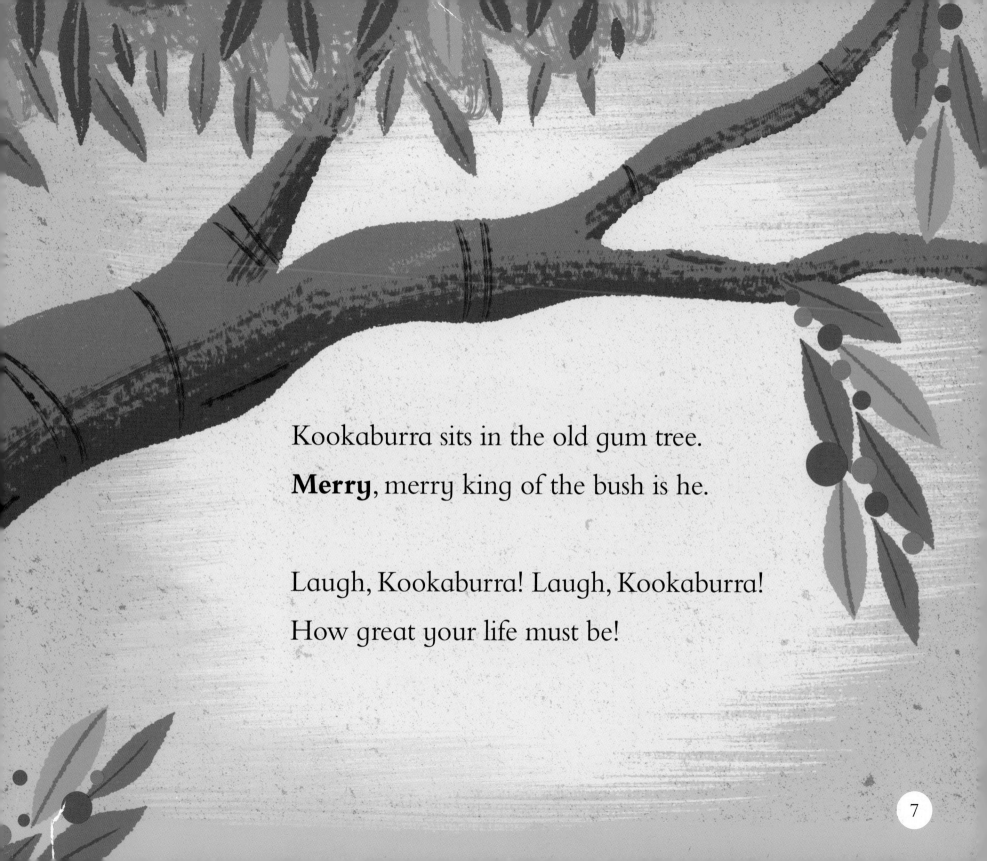

Kookaburra sits in the old gum tree.
Merry, merry king of the bush is he.

Laugh, Kookaburra! Laugh, Kookaburra!
How great your life must be!

Kookaburra sits in the old gum tree.

Merry, merry, merry little bird is he.

Sing, Kookaburra! Sing, Kookaburra!

Sing your song for me.

Kookaburra sits in the old gum tree.

Eating all the **gumdrops** he can see.

Stop, Kookaburra! Stop, Kookaburra!

Leave some there for me!

Kookaburra sits in the old gum tree.

Counting all the monkeys he can see.

Stop, Kookaburra! Stop, Kookaburra!

That's not a monkey. That's me.

Kookaburra sits in the old gum tree.

Merry, merry king of the bush is he.

Laugh, Kookaburra! Laugh, Kookaburra!

How great your life must be!

15

Kookaburra sits in the old gum tree.

Merry, merry, merry little bird is he.

Sing, Kookaburra! Sing, Kookaburra!

Sing your song for me.

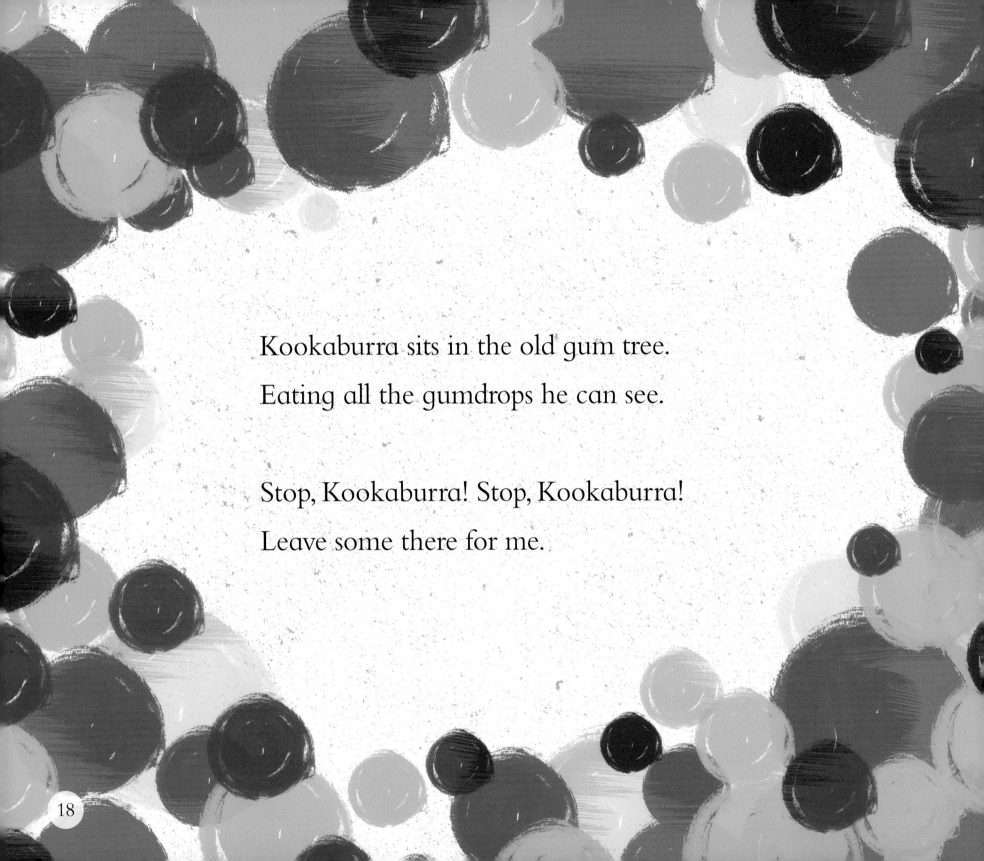

Kookaburra sits in the old gum tree.

Eating all the gumdrops he can see.

Stop, Kookaburra! Stop, Kookaburra!

Leave some there for me.

Kookaburra sits in the old gum tree.
Counting all the monkeys he can see.

Stop, Kookaburra! Stop, Kookaburra!
That's not a monkey. That's me.

SONG LYRICS
Kookaburra

Kookaburra sits in the old gum tree.
Merry, merry king of the bush is he.

Laugh, Kookaburra! Laugh, Kookaburra!
How great your life must be!

Kookaburra sits in the old gum tree.
Merry, merry, merry little bird is he.

Sing, Kookaburra! Sing, Kookaburra!
Sing your song for me.

Kookaburra sits in the old gum tree.
Eating all the gumdrops he can see.

Stop, Kookaburra! Stop, Kookaburra!
Leave some there for me!

Kookaburra sits in the old gum tree.
Counting all the monkeys he can see.

Stop, Kookaburra! Stop, Kookaburra!
That's not a monkey. That's me.

Kookaburra sits in the old gum tree.
Merry, merry king of the bush is he.

Laugh, Kookaburra! Laugh, Kookaburra!
How great your life must be!

Kookaburra sits in the old gum tree.
Merry, merry, merry little bird is he.

Sing, Kookaburra! Sing, Kookaburra!
Sing your song for me.

Kookaburra sits in the old gum tree.
Eating all the gumdrops he can see.

Stop, Kookaburra! Stop, Kookaburra!
Leave some there for me.

Kookaburra sits in the old gum tree.
Counting all the monkeys he can see.

Stop, Kookaburra! Stop, Kookaburra!
That's not a monkey. That's me.

Kookaburra

Americana
Steven C Music

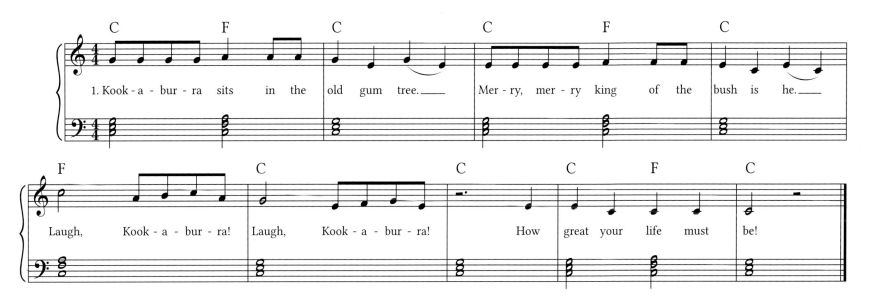

1. Kook - a - bur - ra sits in the old gum tree.___ Mer - ry, mer - ry king of the bush is he.___

Laugh, Kook - a - bur - ra! Laugh, Kook - a - bur - ra! How great your life must be!

Verse 2
Kookaburra sits in the old gum tree.
Merry, merry, merry little bird is he.
Sing, Kookaburra! Sing, Kookaburra!
Sing your song for me.

Verse 3
Kookaburra sits in the old gum tree.
Eating all the gumdrops he can see.
Stop, Kookaburra! Stop, Kookaburra!
Leave some there for me!

Verse 4
Kookaburra sits in the old gum tree.
Counting all the monkeys he can see.
Stop, Kookaburra! Stop, Kookaburra!
That's not a monkey. That's me.

Verse 5
Kookaburra sits in the old gum tree.
Merry, merry king of the bush is he.
Laugh, Kookaburra! Laugh, Kookaburra!
How great your life must be!

Verse 6
Kookaburra sits in the old gum tree.
Merry, merry, merry little bird is he.
Sing, Kookaburra! Sing, Kookaburra!
Sing your song for me.

Verse 7
Kookaburra sits in the old gum tree.
Eating all the gumdrops he can see.
Stop, Kookaburra! Stop, Kookaburra!
Leave some there for me.

Verse 8
Kookaburra sits in the old gum tree.
Counting all the monkeys he can see.
Stop, Kookaburra! Stop, Kookaburra!
That's not a monkey. That's me.

GLOSSARY

Australia—a country that includes the continent of Australia, the island of Tasmania, and several smaller islands

call—the sound a bird makes

gumdrop—a sugar-coated chewy candy

merry—happy and cheerful

New Guinea—an island nation in the southwest Pacific Ocean

GUIDED READING ACTIVITIES

1. What is a kookaburra? Where do kookaburras live? Draw a picture of where they live.

2. What do you think a kookaburra sounds like?

3. What does the kookaburra eat in this story? Do you think kookaburras really eat that? If not, make a hypothesis, or a guess, about what they eat. Find a nonfiction book about kookaburras and research what they eat.

TO LEARN MORE

Allgor, Marie. *Endangered Animals of Australia*. New York: PowerKids Press, 2011.

Ganeri, Anita. *Australia*. Chicago: Heinemann Library, 2014.

Kras, Sara Louise. *Koalas*. Mankato, MN: Capstone Press, 2010.

Ward, Chris. *Discover Australia*. New York: PowerKids Press, 2012.

1 CD